'Prizes!' said Wallace. 'Ooh, yes! – I'll go in for that.

Entering a picture competition in the local village festival, Wallace discovers that an awful lot of other things get covered in paint as well as his picture. And then when his little brother, Henry, wanders outside with his paint-brush in his hand, it seems as though they might be entering the competition for the best-decorated house as well!

An imaginary wolf in the garden shed, an escaped horse which has to be taken home, magic chickens laying Easter eggs and great hairy, striped caterpillars are just a few of the exciting things that come into Wallace's life.

These delightful and funny stories have been specially written for very young children, who will find that they have a lot in common with the enterprising Wallace!

You can read more stories about Wallace and Henry in THE NEW RED BIKE AND OTHER STORIES by Simon Watson, which is also published in Young Puffins.

Simon Watson has written six books for children. He is married with two sons, and is Head of English at a boys' school in Hertfordshire.

The Picture Prize
and Other Stories for the very Young

Simon Watson

Illustrated by Charlotte Voake

PUFFIN BOOKS

Puffin Books, Penguin Books Ltd, Harmondsworth, Middlesex, England
Viking Penguin Inc., 40 West 23rd Street, New York, New York 10010, U.S.A.
Penguin Books Australia Ltd, Ringwood, Victoria, Australia
Penguin Books Canada Limited, 2801 John Street, Markham, Ontario, Canada L3R 1B4
Penguin Books (N.Z.) Ltd, 182–190 Wairau Road, Auckland 10, New Zealand

First published by William Heinemann Ltd. 1981
Published in Puffin Books 1986

Made and printed in Great Britain by
Richard Clay (The Chaucer Press) Ltd, Bungay, Suffolk

Contents

To Adam and Henry

Wallace Loses a Tooth

"What are you eating, Daddy?" asked Wallace as they walked along one day.

"A piece of chewing gum," said Daddy. "I found it in Mummy's pocket."

"Can I have some?" said Wallace.

"No."

"Can *I* have some?" said Henry. Henry was Wallace's younger brother.

"No."

Then all of a sudden Daddy stopped and put his hand up to his mouth. "Oh crikey!" he said, "that's done it!"

"What?" said Wallace.

"I've lost a filling," said Daddy. "That'll serve me right for chewing chewing-gum."

"A filling?" said Wallace. "You mean one of those grey things in your teeth? Can we see?"

Daddy took the gum out of his mouth and showed Wallace and Henry the grey bits in it. Then they took it in turns to look into Daddy's mouth.

"All those grey things are fillings?" said Wallace.

"That's right."

"And the dentist put them in, did he?" said Wallace.

"Yes," said Daddy. "Now he'll have to put a new one in here — socking great hole it is."

"Well, that's all right," said Mummy when they got home, "the boys are going to the dentist next week anyway — you can take them."

So off they all went. But first they cleaned their teeth. Of course they cleaned their teeth every night before going to bed, though it was a nuisance. And sometimes there was trouble about it: Henry insisted on squeezing his own paste and often took too much which then fell off the brush. Also he was just learning to spit: Daddy gave him a good mouthful of water and Henry swilled it round but then instead of spitting it out he swallowed it, or it dribbled out and down his dressing-gown. Sometimes Wallace refused to come and Daddy would have to say, "Very well: no teeth-clean — no sweets."

So they had a good brush now so that the dentist should be pleased with them.

Whey they got to the dentist's they rang the bell and walked up the steep stairs. There was a lady in a white coat who showed them into the waiting room.

"There's plenty to read," said Daddy, pointing to the magazines on the table. But Wallace and Henry squabbled and wriggled for room to sit on Daddy.

"What does that say?" said Wallace. He was pointing at a notice on the wall — a picture of two children eating lollipops.

"It says it's bad for your teeth to eat too many

sweets," said Daddy.

"Oh!" said Wallace.

Then it was their turn to go into the dentist. Daddy was the first into the chair. It was a long chair and it sloped backwards. There was a big light overhead which the dentist brought down to shine into Daddy's face. Then the dentist started picking about in Daddy's mouth.

"We've cleaned our teeth," said Wallace.

"Good," said the dentist. "Now I'm going to use my drill." And he held into Daddy's mouth a thing a bit like a thick pen on the end of a wire; it made a whizzing noise.

Soon Daddy's filling was done and then it was Wallace's turn.

"It didn't hurt, did it, Dad?" said Wallace.

"Not a bit," said Daddy.

But Wallace didn't fancy being in that enormous chair all by himself with the light in his eyes, so he sat on Daddy. The dentist's face came very close to him as he held his mouth as wide open as it could go. It was all over in no time.

"I expect you'll be losing some of those teeth soon," said the dentist, "— at your age."

"And the fairies will give you some money," said Daddy.

Henry went up after Wallace and they were soon all three finished and ready to go.

"Try and keep the sweets down to once a week," said the dentist.

"Oh dear! Yes," said Daddy.

They put their coats on at the top of the stairs and then Wallace did a funny thing. He fell down — all the way down, and not just bump-bump on his bottom but head-over-heels, as in a funny film.

Wallace was a bit surprised when he found himself at the foot of the stairs.

"Are you all right?" said Daddy, who looked a bit worried.

When Wallace realised what had happened he thought he might cry but be found he didn't really want to. He wasn't actually hurt — except his bottom lip a bit — just a little bumped and surprised.

"Good boy," said Daddy, "you deserve a sweet for that ... oh no! Perhaps not, after what the dentist said. I know what ..."

And they went out and Daddy bought a couple of juicy apples.

They were just about to get into the car, Wallace and Henry munching away, when Wallace let out a squawk and pointed at his apple with his mouth full.

"What is it?" said Daddy. "Have you found a caterpillar?"

Wallace shook his head and made as if to spit out the chewed bits. Daddy quickly collected them in his hand.

"It's not a caterpillar," said Wallace, "it's a stone."

Daddy looked carefully at the bits.

"There's no stone here," he said. "I'll tell you what there is, though — look." And he held something white between his finger and thumb. "It's a tooth — *your* tooth. Open your mouth Wallace — let's look."

Sure enough there was a gap — right in the middle of his bottom row.

"Look, Mum," said Wallace when they got home, and he grinned at her to show his gap.

It was good having that gap. Wallace could stick the front bit of his tongue through it; he could fix a straw in it and in the bath he could nearly squirt water through it.

He had his tooth wrapped up in paper and that night he put it under his pillow for the fairies. In the morning he found the tooth gone and a ten p. piece in its place.

He ran into Mummy's room.

"Mummy, how many teeth have I got?"

"Twenty — I think," said Mummy.

"Twenty!" said Wallace. "Coo! that's a *lot* of money," he said, and ran off to put the ten p. in his money box.

In a minute he was back.

"Another thing, Mummy," he said, "that's one less tooth to clean!"

The Wolf in the Shed

At the end of the garden next to the wood was an old black shed with ivy growing on it.

"What's in there?" asked Joanna.

"Daddy says we can't go in," said Wallace, "because it's old and might fall down on top of us."

Joanna went to the door to try it but there was a big metal pole across it so that it couldn't be opened.

"It might be a tramp living in there," she said.

"Or Father Christmas," said Henry.

"Daddy says it's just sticks and old bicycles," said Wallace, "and he's going to pull it down if it doesn't fall down first."

"*I* think," said Joanna, "what I *really* think is it's a *wolf* in there — a wolf come in from the wood."

"Well, I'm going to look through the window," said Wallace bravely.

There was a bit of old fencing leaning against the wall so Wallace could quite easily climb up to the dirty glass. He only had a quick look.

"I saw something grey in there," he said.

They all ran away.

They sat on the back doorstep and Wallace said, "I know — let's leave something for it to eat."

So Mummy gave them the pork fat that they were

going to hang up for the birds and they laid it quickly on the window sill of the shed without looking in.

"If it goes," said Wallace, "we'll know there *is* a wolf in there."

They went to play in the house for a while where they couldn't see the shed. They had such a good time playing with the fort that they forgot about the fat and the wolf.

Joanna remembered the next day she came to play with Wallace. "Has it gone?" she said. They ran to look. The fat *had* gone.

They walked quietly away from the shed.

"There *is* a wolf in there, then," said Wallace. Then they saw Henry up the schumack tree. "What are you doing, Henry?" Joanna asked.

"Putting the fat for the birds," said Henry. Wallace and Joanna ran to look.

"Weren't you afraid of the wolf, Henry?" said Wallace.

"He didn't want it," said Henry.

"Perhaps there isn't a wolf after all," said Wallace.

"*I* think there is," said Joanna. "I think I've heard him from my house at night — barking."

Wallace began to think about the wolf when he went to bed.

"Daddy," he said, "are there wolves in England?"

"No," said Daddy, "not any more — none at all. There used to be, a long time ago."

"In the olden times," said Wallace.

But as he went to sleep he listened for the wolf in the shed. There *was* a barking. Although there weren't any wolves in England any more there could have been *one* left behind.

There was a loud wind blowing. Wallace could hear the trees tangling. Suppose the wind blew the shed down and the wolf escaped?

Wallace got out of bed and ran along to Mummy and Daddy who were watching television. He didn't say what the matter was but they told him he could sleep in their bed. That was better: he could hear the telly more than the wind and the barking.

In the morning Daddy said, "Well, that's done it."

"What?" said Wallace.

"The wind in the night — it's blown the shed down."

Wallace ran to look and there it was — not completely flattened but all on one side and the door had burst off so that you could see in. There was nothing inside but dry wood, a bicycle frame and a broken chair.

"What a bonfire this is going to make!" said Daddy, and he began to smash up the old shed.

"Do you think there could have been a wolf in there, Dad?" said Wallace as he helped.

"No," said Daddy, "wolves don't live in sheds — they live in forests."

Wallace looked out of the garden into the woods.

"This'll go like nobody's business," said Daddy, gathering a pile of wood together. And it did: in no time at all the small flame from a match had grown into a pack of monsters roaring at the wood.

Henry threw on a stick. "Go away, wolves," he said.

Wallace thought, Perhaps the wolf escaped when the shed fell down. Perhaps it's gone to live in the woods.

But the fire burnt hot and high and its flames licked like tongues fiercer than any wolves. And Wallace danced around it.

A Boating Afternoon

"I've got presents for you boys," Daddy said when he came back from a few days away.

The presents were two yellow boats, both exactly the same except for the colour inside: Wallace had the green and Henry the blue. The boats had masts and sails and they floated very well in the bath. But they hadn't got keels like Wallace's other boat.

"They would blow over in a wind, I expect," said Wallace. But the boats were so wide and flat-bottomed that even if you tipped them right over they came upright again. "Mum, could we try them on the paddling pool at Granny's recreation ground when we go?"

"Good idea," said Mummy.

So when they next went to Granny's they took their boats. But there was a disappointment: the pool at the recreation ground was empty.

"I expect they're going to clean it," said Daddy. "Never mind — there isn't much breeze to sail the boats anyway."

"Let's go and watch the big boats on the river instead," said Mummy.

"Can we *go* in a boat?" said Wallace.

"Not today, I don't think."

They walked to the river and stood on the foot-bridge watching a rowing boat or two going underneath.

"Could we sail our boats on the river, Dad?" Wallace asked.

"Well, they might sail away downstream."

"We could have them on a string," said Wallace.

"If we *had* any string," said Daddy.

"What about the string of that kite that won't work," said Mummy. "I think that's in the car."

Wallace ran to get it.

"Do you think it'll be strong enough?" he asked.

"Strong enough for a kite," said Daddy, "should be strong enough for a boat."

So they tied it on. Then Wallace stayed on one bank close to the bridge and Daddy took the string over the bridge and down onto the other side. That way the string stretched right across the river. Then Wallace let go the boat and Daddy pulled. The little yellow boat bobbed beautifully across the river. It floated downstream a bit but came in safe and sound and Wallace ran over to collect it.

"I'll pull next time, Dad," he said and went back over the bridge with the string. Daddy let go the boat and Wallace pulled.

Suddenly Wallace was pulling and the string wasn't coming in and the boat was drifting gently downstream.

"Pull, Wallace!" Mummy shouted.

"I am!" said Wallace. "It won't come!" And he pulled harder.

"Must be caught on something under the water," said Daddy.

Then Wallace fell over backwards: the string was broken. And there was the boat, loose, now drifting away.

"Don't worry, Wallace," said Daddy, "it'll sail into the bank soon."

But it didn't. The current was stronger than the breeze and the boat floated sideways downstream. Daddy followed it but he soon came to a fence with nettles going right down to the water.

"There's only one thing for it," said Mummy, as they watched the yellow boat approaching a bend in the river, "we'll have to go after it in a rowing boat."

"We might never catch up with it," Daddy said.

"We will if you hurry," said Mummy. "The boat-hire place isn't far."

Daddy ran off.

Soon he was back with the rowing boat, the oars dripping water onto his trousers. They all got in and off they went downstream, everyone looking for the little yellow boat.

Daddy didn't row very straight and he got cross because Mummy said he should stay close to one bank and Wallace said he should stay close to another. And Henry wanted to run up and down the boat in a dangerous way. Then just as Wallace was beginning to get upset because he'd never see his boat again, he

spotted it. It had drifted into the bank — the bank *he* told Daddy to stay close to — and was bobbing up and down like a yellow duck among the reeds.

"Well, pity we haven't got a picnic now we're here," said Daddy, when they had collected Wallace's boat, and everyone had calmed down and cheered up.

"Tea-place a little further on," said Mummy.

So they went there and had a big tea. And on the way back Wallace and Henry trailed their boats, one on each side of the rowing boat — on short and double strings.

The Picture Prize

"What shall we do for the village festival?" Mummy asked. "Shall we decorate the house and garden?"

"Ooh, yes!" said Wallace. "Daddy could paint the house all different colours."

"I think we'd need flags and streamers and things," said Mummy.

"We could put Christmas paper-chains on the front gate," said Wallace.

Mummy wasn't so keen on the decorating idea.

"What about entering the picture competition, Wallace," she said. "'The best picture by an under six-year-old: Prizes'."

"Prizes!" said Wallace. "Ooh, yes! — I'll go in for that. Come on, Mum, let's get the paints out."

Mummy groaned. "Must you paint?" she said. "You make such a dreadful mess."

"We'll be careful," said Wallace.

"Won't felt tips do?" asked Mummy.

"We want to paint," said Wallace.

Mummy sighed and got out the paints. She mixed the colours in the little plastic pots, while Wallace got the brushes and Henry put on his apron.

"Roll up your sleeves, both of you," said Mummy. She covered the kitchen table with newspaper.

Soon Wallace and Henry were at work. Wallace was doing a picture of Uncle Christopher, who was a soldier, in red, white and blue.

Henry was just doing colours. He got some of all the colours with the thickest brush and sploshed them all together very wetly in one little patch on his piece of paper.

It was a good painting session but Mummy didn't seem so pleased.

"Oh heavens, Henry! *Look* at you," she said. "You've got paint in your hair — *how* have you managed to get it in your *hair*?"

"I don't know," said Henry, putting his blue and red hand up to his hair to feel it.

"*Don't!*" said Mummy. "And look — oh Henry! —

on your shoes: there's a great blob on your new shoes. This is ridiculous."

"*And* he's got it on his jersey," said Wallace, "his sleeve's come down."

"That's enough painting for *you* today," said Mummy, and dragged Henry off to wash him. Henry kicked and cried. He had been enjoying his painting.

"You make a mess of the table, you make a mess of your clothes, a mess of the floor — it's just too much. You can go outside, both of you."

"Could we paint outside?" said Wallace.

"*I* want to paint outside," said Henry.

"We could paint on the terrace," said Wallace.

"The paper would blow away," said Mummy.

"No, I mean we could paint *on* the terrace — on the stone squares."

"That *is* a good idea," said Mummy. She took off Henry's shoes and all his clothes except his pants and he was ready.

On the terrace Wallace and Henry got to work on their different squares. They used lots of paint. Mummy brought them more. Henry was a bit of trouble treading where Wallace was painting. After a while he wandered off to paint the wall.

Then Mummy came out and had a go too. She wrote Wallace's name in big letters, one letter in each square, each letter a different colour. "They could see that from an aeroplane," said Wallace. Then Mummy did the days of the week.

"I like this," said Wallace. "Hey Mummy! — perhaps we could go in for the best decorated house and garden with this."

"Oh! I don't think this would be enough," said Mummy. "By the way, where's Henry?"

"I don't know," said Wallace, "busy somewhere, I expect."

Mummy went inside. After a while Wallace *did* wonder where Henry had got to. He saw that he had done some painting on the wall; he had even had a little go at their tree.

Wallace went round to the front of the house. There was a trail of blue drops along the path. Then Wallace stopped.

"Blimey!" he exlaimed.

Henry had been busy, all right. He had painted half the back bumper of the car blue, he had painted the gatepost blue; he had painted some of the bars of the gate and he had painted the name of the house. He now had paint on his face as well as in his hair. In fact, he had some paint on pretty well all of his body.

"Cor! Henry!" said Wallace, and he dashed off to get the red and the white. "Soldier colours," he said, "red, white and blue. Come on Henry."

And they set to work. First they painted the bars of the gate alternately red, white and blue. Of course, they couldn't do it *all*, but they did a lot of it.

Then they set to work on the stones at the edge of the flowerbed: alternately red, white and blue. And when they'd done enough of that Wallace painted Henry red, white and blue. He couldn't do him all because it tickled but Wallace was pleased with what he'd done. "I think I'll enter *you* for the competition, Henry," he said.

Then Mummy came out. She was holding Wallace's painting of Uncle Christopher. "Wallace," she said, "this is a really good picture." Then she saw Henry, and the gate — and the stones. For a moment she didn't say anything. Then she laughed.

Then Daddy got the paddling pool out and Wallace and Henry had a good splash to get the paint off.

"The rain'll wash the paint off the gate and the stones," said Daddy.

"We don't *want* it to come off," said Wallace. "Do we, Henry? Henry might win the prize for the best decorated house and garden."

"Mmm," said Daddy.

"Well, I shouldn't be surprised if Wallace won the picture competition," said Mummy.

"What's the prize?" asked Wallace.

Mummy didn't know.

The judges smiled when they saw what Wallace and Henry had done. One of them nodded to the other and asked the boys their names and ages.

"I don't think we've won, Henry," said Wallace when the judges had gone.

But they all went to the prize-giving at the school in the evening and Wallace won a prize for his painting — first prize.

"What is it?" Mummy asked.

"Felt pens," said Wallace, disappointed. But Mummy thought that was a good prize.

When it came to the best decorated house and

garden competition, Wallace and Henry *hadn't* won first prize. They hadn't won second or third either. But after those prizes had been announced the judges said, "A special prize goes to the youngest contestants in the competition." And he read out Wallace's and Henry's names and ages. Both the boys went up to collect the prize.

"This is more like it," said Wallace, when they opened it.

"Why, what is it this time?" Mummy asked.

Wallace waved it triumphantly in the air. "A box of paints!" he cried.

Wallace Rides a Horse

One day Mummy and Wallace were just coming home from shopping when Mummy stopped the car outside the gate to their house.

"Good gracious! Look at that, Wallace," said Mummy.

Wallace had been lying on the back seat, singing. He sat up and looked. "It's a horse," he said.

And it was: just calmly walking out of their front gate into the road was a fat grey pony. It looked at them and then began munching the grass alongside their fence.

The man from the garage came along and said, "Better call the police. Whose horse is it? Where does it come from?"

"I think it probably comes from the field behind our house," said Mummy.

"It could cause an accident out here," said the garage man.

"I'll catch it," said Mummy, and they drove the car into the drive — slowly, so as not to frighten the pony.

Mummy went in and got one of Daddy's belts. "This'll hold him," she said.

The pony was very quiet and Mummy easily put the belt round its neck.

"Come on, little fat grey," she said, "you come and wait in the garden." And she led him back behind the house where she tethered him to the clothes-line tree. The pony began happily to munch the grass.

"Oh! look what he's done," said Wallace. The pony had made a big pile on the path.

"Never mind," said Mummy. "Daddy'll like that for the garden. Oh dear! what is he doing now?"

The pony had got caught up in the washing line and had pulled it to the ground.

"Having a bit of trouble, dear?" came a big voice from behind, and there was a policeman wearing a cap.

"I think he came in through the hedge at the bottom of the garden," said Mummy, and they all went to have a look.

"Yes, that looks like it," said the policeman. They could all see a big gap and hoof marks on the garden side of it.

Then two more policemen arrived. They all looked at the pony. One of them got out a note-book and said to Mummy, "Would you say that was a boy or a girl now, dear?"

"Boy," said Mummy.

"What sort of age do you think that would be, dear?"

Mummy answered all the policeman's questions. "I'll take the horse back," she said.

"Thanks, dear," the policeman said. Then all

three policemen got into the car and Wallace watched them drive away.

"Well, Wallace," said Mummy, "we'll take him back, shall we? We'll have to go round by the road." Mummy untethered him and began to lead him out of the garden. "You're a nice peaceful chap," she said to the pony. "Hey, Wallace, do you think you'd like to ride him?"

"Oh yes, please!" said Wallace. So Mummy put him up and Wallace held onto the mane and had a lovely ride all the way down the pavement past Katie's house, down the rough road past Stephen's house and up to the gate in the field where the pony belonged.

"Oh dear! It's locked," said Mummy, but just then a girl came up. It was her pony. She said she was sorry the pony had come into their garden but he was very greedy and always looking about for more food. His name was Caesar.

Mummy and Wallace said goodbye to Ceasar and watched him being put back in his field.

"Can we have a horse of our own?" said Wallace.

"Not now," said Mummy. "Perhaps one day — when you're bigger."

"But I *am* bigger," said Wallace.

"But not big enough," said Mummy. "Come on — we'd better go and mend that hole in the fence before Caesar gets through again."

And off they went. As they walked back down the track Wallace saw hoof marks on the ground.

"That was when *I* was riding the pony," he said.

Treasure

"Will you put up my rope ladder, Dad?" asked Wallace.

"And my swing?" said Henry.

"It's certainly fine enough now," said Daddy. It was warm and windy, the daffodils were coming out and Daddy was getting ready to dig.

So soon Wallace was climbing and swinging on his rope ladder. Henry had his space-hat on as well as his shorts and he was swinging too. Wallace wanted Daddy to watch him catch the apple tree branches between his legs as he swung.

After a while they went to see how Daddy was getting on.

"I've just put in a row of carrots," said Daddy.

"Can *we* have gardens?" said Wallace.

"Like last year?" said Daddy. "Yes."

"I'll get a cultivator," said Wallace.

"I'll get a rake," said Henry.

Soon they were hard at work. Henry wanted carrots and lettuces; Wallace wanted carrots and cabbages.

Daddy prepared the ground and made little drills for them to put the seed in. Henry had trouble with the seed. It spilled out of his hand and too many of the seeds didn't go into the drill. "The birds'll get those," said Daddy. "Never mind."

Wallace had chosen pelleted seeds for his cabbages. They had a special packet and they came out of a little hole one at a time. Wallace put them in the drill carefully one inch apart. Then Daddy riddled earth over the drills to cover them up.

"Let's just hope Wussy doesn't use *this* spot," he said.

The next day, while Daddy was digging again, Wallace and Henry came running up.

"Look what Henry's found!"

"It's a penny," said Daddy. "An old penny. Why don't you see if you can find some more."

Wallace and Henry ran off but soon came back; they couldn't find any more.

Mummy came out. "I suppose we've finished all the potatoes," she said.

"Oh yes!" said Daddy.

"Well, I'll be off to the shop then, to get some more," said Mummy. "Anyone coming?"

"No thanks," said Wallace. "We're digging for treasure."

Wallace got the fork and started. It was hard work getting it into the ground. After pushing on the handle with both hands he had to jump on each shoulder of the fork in turn to get it in. When it was right in he had to pull as hard as he could on it to get the earth up. It was a big lump of earth but there was no treasure in it or under it.

"I don't think there's much treasure here, Dad,"
said Wallace. "I think I'll try somewhere else."

"Try over there — that bumpy bit," Daddy sug-
gested. "That's where Henry had his potatoes last
year. The earth'll be softer there."

It was too. Wallace soon had a forkful up.

"Cor! Dad, look what I've found."

"A potato!" said Henry.

"That's right, Henry," said Daddy, "you grew
that potato last year. It got left behind. And it's
all right too — not rotten. See if you can find some
more to give Mummy — she needn't have gone
shopping."

Wallace dug very busily again but he couldn't

find any more potatoes. Or any other kind of treasure.

"To find treasure you have to bury it first," said Daddy. "That'll be your treasure, Wallace." He pointed at Wallace's row of carrots. "You can dig them up in the summer."

"Not very exciting treasure," said Wallace.

Henry had gone to chase Wussy off his lettuce seeds and through the hedge. He said, "I've found gold."

Wallace ran over. "Daddy, it *is* gold — *really* — come and look."

Daddy went. There amongst the dead leaves under the hedge Henry had found a gold coin. It wasn't dull like the penny — it was really shiny gold, a bit dirty but definitely gold. It seemed a bit bent and bashed, though.

"Well, I'm blowed," said Daddy. "Do you know what that is? It's left over from your pirate party. You remember I hid them — the coins — all over the garden for you to find? You missed this one. It's *chocolate* gold."

Daddy carefully unpeeled the side of the coin and they could see inside — well, it *was* sort of chocolate. "Amazing it's lasted," said Daddy.

A penny someone had once dropped; a potato that had missed being dug up; a pirate's gold coin that had lain all winter under the hedge. A year's treasure.

Wallace began digging again.

"Decided to look for more, have you, Wallace?" asked Daddy.

"No," Wallace replied, "I'm going to bury this."

Into the hole they went — penny, potato, pirate's gold — deep into the ground: treasure for the future.

Hairwash Night

Wallace and Henry were in the bath.

"Hairwash night tonight," said Mummy.

"Oh no!" said Wallace.

"Oh yes!" said Mummy. "And see if you can have it without crying this time, both of you. It really doesn't hurt."

"I don't like soap in my eyes," said Wallace.

"I never get soap in your eyes — only water," Mummy replied.

"Can't we play first?" asked Henry.

"All right," said Mummy, "for a while."

Wallace and Henry had a good play. Wallace was pouring water with yoghurt cartons while Henry had the face flannel mitten with the hippo on: he was stuffing his soldiers into it. Then he watered the cow that was standing on the edge of the bath; a lot of the water went onto the floor. Wallace used his cartons to fill the jug at his end of the bath: he stood up and poured from a height. Quite a lot of that water went onto the floor too.

Then Wallace started squirting water from his mouth. He filled a yoghurt carton with fresh cold water from the tap and, taking a mouthful, he squirted it at Henry. Henry didn't like it at first but Wallace gave him a carton of his own to squirt Wallace with and that was fine.

When Mummy came back to the bathroom she was so angry at the mess on the floor and the silly spitting that she forgot about the hairwash. She yanked them both out of the bath and spanked them along to dry in front of the fire in their room.

But next night she had remembered.

"Right — who's first for hairwash?" she said.

"Not me," said Wallace.

"Not me," said Henry.

"Well, it's one of you," said Mummy. "Wallace, I think it's you."

"I think it's Henry," said Wallace.

"No!" Henry shouted and splashed his cup down on the water.

"Five minutes to play," said Mummy, "then I'm coming back to wash *somebody's* hair."

"Not mine," said Wallace.

"Not me," said Henry.

"And this time keep the water in the bath," said Mummy, and she went out.

"We're not going to have our hair washed, are we, Henry?" said Wallace.

"No," said Henry and they had a nice time pouring water about. Henry held the jug and Wallace stood up and poured water down into it from a carton. It splashed off the bottom at first but soon Wallace had it half full.

"Hold it still, Henry," he said.

But the next cupful Wallace poured missed the

jug and went over the front of Henry's hair. Henry spluttered and began to cry. "Mummy!" he wailed.

"It's all right, Henry," said Wallace quickly. "Look — look at me," and he took a carton full of water and poured it down on his own head. He meant to get just a little on his hair but his hand slipped again and it went over most of his head. He spluttered and tried to sit down but he'd closed his eyes to keep the water out and trod on Henry's leg by mistake so that he slipped and fell into the water, banging his head on the side of the bath and getting completely wet.

Henry laughed. Wallace wiped the water out of his eyes.

"Shall I do that to you?" Wallace asked Henry.

"No," said Henry. "Look at me."

Henry took a jug and emptied the water out of it over his own head so that *he* was soaked as well; but it was more than he had expected and *he* was spluttering and wiping the water out of his eyes too.

At that moment Mummy came in again.

"Ah!" she said, "ready for hairwash, I see — nicely wetted hair? On with the shampoo, then," and before they knew where they were Mummy was working both their scalps into soapy lighthouses.

And when it came to lying back and being rinsed neither of them complained at all.

"You've had your hair washed?" said Daddy in surprise when they came down to supper. "But I didn't hear a cry."

"Oh! we don't mind having our hair washed, do we, Henry?"

"No," said Henry, "we don't mind water all over us."

"Not even in our eyes," said Wallace.

Wallace's Toolbox

Wallace liked to help Daddy in the house if Daddy was working with his drill and his screwdriver and other tools.

The trouble was Wallace used to borrow Daddy's tools when Daddy wasn't there and things got lost.

"*All* my nails have gone, Wallace," Daddy complained one day. And he hid his toolbag where Wallace couldn't get it.

But for his birthday Wallace got a toolbox of his own. It had a metal screwdriver, a wooden hammer with a round head, a little box of nails, a sandpapering block, and a large metal saw with proper sharp teeth.

"I can help *you* now, Daddy," said Wallace.

"Yes," said Daddy.

"I could build a house with these," said Wallace.

"You could," said Daddy.

Daddy gave Wallace a large bit of softboard for him to saw bits off and hammer nails into. All Wallace's friends liked to work at it too but soon they'd lost all the nails.

"We'll buy you some more," said Mummy. And they went into town and bought a large packet of real workman's nails in an ironmonger's shop — not toy ones from a toy shop. They put the nails in a carton with a lid and kept all the tools in a shoe box held shut with an elastic band.

The next day Wallace and Henry made themselves a bed in the long grass with Wussy. "See me, Dad," said Henry.

"Will you build us a house here?" Wallace asked.

Dad said, "All right — I'll see what materials I've got."

"What's 'materials'?" said Wallace.

"Things to make it with," said Daddy. "We need something for the sides and something for the roof."

"And a door," said Henry.

"And windows," said Wallace.

"Well, we'll see," said Daddy.

First they found the big wooden ladder that Daddy had made for them. They put that on its side for one wall. Then there was a big bit of wood that had once been the top half of the tool-shed door. That made another wall. Daddy hammered stakes alongside the walls to prevent them from falling down.

"Now what about our third wall?" said Daddy.

"I know!" said Wallace, "the old fireguard."

"That's a good idea," said Daddy. "We won't need that any more."

So they collected the old fireguard from the tool-shed. It made a very good end, especially as it had bits of side as well to lengthen the walls.

"We'll just cover that with this old cloth," said Daddy, "and there we are."

"What about the roof?" said Wallace.

"Ah yes!" said Daddy. Then he remembered the two loose doors in the caravan. They did very well, together with a large piece of hardboard that Wallace had had his town layout on.

"Now for the door," said Dad. He found some plastic sacks to hang from the roof down over the end.

"They're cat-flaps," said Wallace, and Wallace and Henry scrambled in and out through them. But they fell off the roof because they were only held down by a piece of wood.

"Soon fix that," said Daddy. "A few nails will hold it . . . Oh dear! I don't think I've *got* any nails that size. And how am I going to fix those planks on the ladder wall without any nails?"

"I've got some nails, Dad," said Wallace. "*I've* got some nails."

"Of course — I'd forgotten," said Daddy. "Can we use them?"

"Yes you can," said Wallace, and he ran off to get his toolbox.

Wallace's nails were just the right size. He and Daddy hammered the sacks down onto the roof so that they didn't fall off every time someone went in or out. And they hammered the planks against the ladder to block up that wall.

"There," said Dad, "there we are — all finished."

Wallace and Henry scrambled in and out. "We're cats," they said.

"I couldn't have done it without your nails, Wallace," said Daddy. "You see — you *did* build a house, didn't you?"

The Magic Chickens

Wallace wasn't in a good mood.

"*Where* are we going?" he asked in a groaning sort of voice, as they drove along.

"To see Richard," said Mummy. "He's an old friend of Daddy's. He lives by himself and he has a farm."

"Oh!" said Wallace. "I don't suppose he's got any toys."

"Might have," said Daddy.

"He might have an Easter egg for us," said Wallace. (Wallace had been given four Easter eggs the day before.)

"Don't be greedy," said Daddy.

But Richard *had* got some toys. He had the best collection of toy soldiers Wallace had ever seen. Richard took Wallace and Henry up to the attic to get them: they were in a big black tin box. And inside that were cardboard boxes with layers of cotton wool; and in the cotton wool lay these soldiers — proper lead soldiers.

Wallace and Henry set them up on the drawing-room table. The best ones were the foreign legion: their bayonets were straight and there wasn't a scratch on them. Wallace put them in marching order. There were drummers in kilts that Richard's mummy had painted when he was a little boy and some tiny First World War soldiers including two stretcher-bearers without a stretcher.

At lunch they had different-coloured jellies in little pots. That was nice, though there was only one sweet each after lunch.

"Haven't you got any Easter eggs?" Wallace asked Richard.

"Wallace!" said Daddy sharply.

"I haven't got any Easter eggs," said Richard, "but I have got some magic chickens."

"Magic chickens?" said Wallace. "Can we see them?"

"Not now," said Richard, "later. It's time to give the bull his lunch."

The bull had a big curly head and he looked quite friendly.

Then they went to see the ducks on the pond. The ducks kept well away from them and the water looked a bit too deep for Wallace's liking. They had to go over a loose-board bridge to get to the island.

"Can we see the dogs?" said Henry.

The dogs were inside Richard's little blue van. When they went up to it the van started shaking the dogs were jumping around so much. When Richard opened the back door two huge black labradors burst out and wagged their tails and bustled round them but didn't jump up.

One of them was the mother of the other. She had four legs but only three of them worked: the

41

fourth just hung and didn't touch the ground even when she walked. "She was run over," said Richard.

There was another little brown dog but that stayed in the car with its nose sticking out of the window.

"Now, have you ever been in a tractor?" Richard asked.

"No," said Wallace and Henry.

"Come on then."

Richard took them to a big shed. Inside it were three new blue tractors. Richard unhitched the trailer of one of them; then he climbed in and turned on the radio and the engine. Wallace and Henry scrambled up and they drove off out of the shed.

When they were in the yard Richard said, "Would you like to have a drive, Wallace?" And he showed Wallace what to do.

Wallace held the wheel with both hands and drove the tractor three times round the yard. Richard helped him a little and then took over to back the tractor into the shed.

"I drove it, Mummy," said Wallace.

"Well done, Wallace," said Mummy. "Well, we must be off home now."

"But we haven't seen the magic chickens yet," said Wallace.

"Come on," said Richard. "But first I must fetch a basket to collect the eggs in."

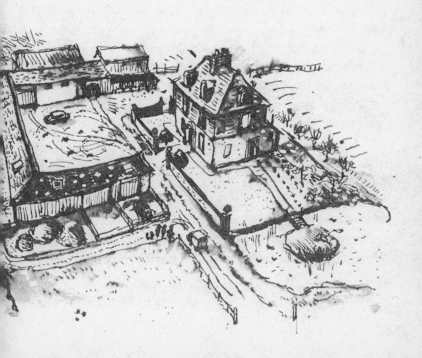

When he came back with the basket, he led them to the chickens' shed. In the shed there was a row of nesting boxes against the wall. The chickens looked like ordinary chickens to Wallace.

"What's magic about them?" he asked.

"You'll see," said Richard, and he put his hand into one of the boxes. "I thought so," he said. "Look in there, Wallace." Richard lifted him up to see.

In the nesting-boxes there were five eggs: two brown, one white and two ... yellow and blue.

"They're *Easter* eggs!" exclaimed Wallace.

"Fetch them all out then" said Richard.

So Wallace put in his hand and brought them out carefully to put in Richard's basket.

"Can *I* find some?" said Henry.

Richard picked Henry up and let him look into the next box.

"Nothing in there," said Henry.

Richard put his hand in the next one to feel for the eggs. "Anything there, Henry?" he said.

"Yellow and red eggs!" said Henry and he picked them out.

Richard gave Mummy and Daddy half a dozen ordinary eggs and Wallace and Henry had two chicken-sized Easter eggs each.

"All right, you can have one each now," said Mummy as they drove away.

"That was pretty good, eh Wallace?" said Daddy. "You said you didn't think Richard would have anything."

"Well, he did," said Wallace, as he bit into his egg. "He had *everything*!"

Wallace and the Caterpillars

One day when Mummy was hanging out the washing she found a caterpillar in a tree by the line. She called Wallace to see.

"That's not a caterpillar," said Wallace, "that's a stick insect."

It didn't have evenly-spaced legs like a caterpillar but four sturdy ones at the back and two smaller ones at the front. When it walked it hunched its back into a loop, bringing its hind legs forward.

"I'll keep this to show Joanna," said Wallace.

They got an empty margarine carton and punched some slits in its lid. Then Wallace gathered a few young leaves off the tree the creature had been feeding on and put them inside the carton for him to eat.

"You'll have to get him fresh leaves every day," said Mummy. "What are you going to call him?"

"Sticky," said Wallace.

The next day he took Sticky to school to show Joanna.

"I wish *I* had a caterpillar," said Joanna. "He's really nice."

In playtime they went round the playground looking for caterpillars on the leaves of the overhanging trees. But they didn't find any.

The very next morning though, Joanna came in with her own margarine carton.

"I've got one, Wallace," she said. "I found it at home."

Joanna's was much more like an ordinary caterpillar. It wasn't as big or as exciting-looking as some in Wallace's book but it had lots of legs and it was bright green.

"I'm calling him Stocky," said Joanna, "because of Sticky."

"Do you think they'd like to be together?" said Wallace. "We could put them both in one carton."

They decided to keep their own ones but their cartons sat side by side during school. Every day Wallace and Joanna got fresh leaves for Sticky and Stocky and cleaned out their cartons.

"My Mummy says we ought to let them go," said Wallace.

"They're all right," said Joanna. "I think they're growing: you can see how much they've eaten."

"Anyway I expect they'll soon turn into chrysalises." said Wallace. "Then the next thing we know they'll be butterflies."

"Or moths," said Joanna.

A few days later they found something really exciting. They were sitting together in school behind Alex when what should they see but an enormous caterpillar making its way over Alex's shoulder. Joanna collected it just in time before Alex saw it. Then she and Wallace inspected it. It was beautiful — not just enormous, but black with scarlet and white on it. It was very hairy too with a little tuft of bristles on each hump, like tiny shaving brushes.

"You might get a rash," said Wallace.

"I don't care," said Joanna. "Now what shall we do with him? Shall we put him in with Sticky or with Stocky?"

"The trouble is," said Wallace, "we don't know what he eats. Not Alex's shirt, I don't think!"

"We could ask Mrs Jones," said Joanna.

"She might tell us to let them go," said Wallace.

So they put him — Stripy they decided to call him — in Stocky's carton, moving Stocky in with Sticky. Wallace took them home and Joanna took Stripy.

She brought Stripy into school the next day in a carton almost bursting with different kinds of leaves. "But he doesn't seem to have eaten any of them," she said, "and he's gone very still."

"Well, Sticky and Stocky are chrysalising," said Wallace. They saw how two of the leaves were curled up and being bound over with furry white thread.

"My Mum says that may mean they are unhappy and are going to die," said Joanna.

"I don't think so," said Wallace. "Anyway what are we going to do about Stripy?"

They didn't know *what* to do. They got some different leaves from around the playground. But by the next day there was still no sign that Stripy had eaten anything.

"You can't say he looks ill," said Wallace. "His hairs aren't drooping or anything."

"But he's not *lively*, is he?" said Joanna. "I think we'll have to let him go. And I think we should let Sticky and Stocky go too — they might change their minds about dying."

"If there *are* dying," said Wallace. "But *where* do we let Stripy go?"

During the day Wallace found the insect book. "Here, there's a picture of it," he told Joanna. "What's it eating? I can't read that word."

They had to ask Mrs Jones. The word was 'lilac'.

"Is there any lilac at school, Mrs Jones?" asked Wallace.

"Yes," said Mrs Jones, "by the gate."

So on the lilac tree by the gate they let Stripy go. And they put Sticky and Stocky on the ground under it, hoping for the best.

The next day they went to look where they had put him. He had gone.

"Look at this, Wallace," Joanna called. She showed Wallace a jagged leaf on the lilac tree. "See — it's been nibbled. I'm sure Stripy's all right."

Wallace hoped so too.

Anyway, there were a lot of butterflies later in the summer.

The Goldfish Pond

Wallace and Henry went to stay in Granny's house for her while she was away.

Under the little beech tree at the bottom of Granny's lawn there was a goldfish pond.

"A goldfish pond!" said Wallace. "I can't see any goldfish. I can't see any water. All I can see is leaves."

"It used to be a pond," said Daddy.

But now it was just quite a wide but not very deep hole in the ground with concrete bottom and sides. It had a little rocky island in the middle.

"Let's fill it up with water," said Wallace. "We could sail our boats in it."

"Go fishing in it," said Henry.

"The water would just leak through the bottom, I'm afraid," said Daddy.

But that night it rained and the pond had a little water in it. Henry fished leaves out of it with his fishing rod and Wallace collected bits of brick to drop in it.

The next day it rained all day long. It was raining when they got up in the morning and it was raining when they went to bed.

The next morning when Wallace looked out of

the window it was more than raining — it was water-falling: water was pouring down past the window as thick as if someone were pouring it from a bucket.

Wallace went into Mummy's and Daddy's room and told Daddy but he wasn't interested. Wallace went back and watched the waterfall. It was pattering on the window ledge outside and there were huge puddles in the drive, some of them too wide to jump across.

In the end Daddy came in. "Crikey!" he said, "I see what you mean about a waterfall! The gutter must be blocked."

So they all got into their boots and their wet-suits and went out to investigate.

Daddy got the ladder and climbed up it to reach the gutter. Soon he was chucking down great clots of leaves and the water was gurgling out of the drain-pipe beside Wallace and Henry. The little drain pool soon filled up. Wallace cleared it of leaves and the water ran away.

During breakfast the rain stopped and they went out again. Everything was sopping and the tub by the greenhouse was brimming over.

"*Look* at the goldfish pond!" said Wallace. "It's a lake!"

It was full and overflowing the sides onto the lawn. The grass was standing up in inches of water and the island was only just showing above the water.

"You could almost *swim* in that," said Wallace.

"Why don't you get your boats?" said Daddy. Henry was already fishing splashily.

"No, I know!" said Wallace. "The box! That could be a boat — come on, Dad!"

So they went off to the shed to get the box. Daddy called it a crate. It had writing on the sides and it was so big that when Henry stood inside he could only just see out.

They lugged the box over to the pond and heaved it onto the water. "It floats!" said Wallace as the box bobbed across to the island.

"Can I have a ride in it?" asked Wallace.

Daddy stepped into the pond — it was nearly over the top of his boots — and held the box at the edge

for Wallace to climb into. Then he swung the box about in the water. It tipped and Wallace clung on to one side to stop himself falling over backwards and out the other side. Daddy stood on the island and swung the boat sometimes from one end of the pond to the other, sometimes all round the island in a circle. Sometimes he bounced the boat up and down so that a great wash flowed out in ripples onto the lawn and then flowed back into the pond again. Sometimes he twizzled it round in the water so that Wallace got dizzy and didn't know *where* to hold on to and in the end just sat in the sloshy bottom, giggling. Then it was Henry's turn and he got a bit wet because the boat tipped over so much that water rushed in. Then it was Wallace's turn again, then Henry's.

"My turn now," said Wallace.

"No more," said Daddy, "my hands are sore, my socks are wet and I want a cup of coffee."

So they went in.

"That was good, that was," said Wallace. "Can we do it again this afternoon?"

"We'll see," said Daddy.

When they went out in the afternoon the lawn was making sucking noises and the goldfish pond was nearly half empty. The box boat could float by itself but when Wallace got in it bumped against the sides and the bottom too much to make a good ride. They had to leave it.

The next day the sun was shining and in the goldfish pond the box was stranded half against the side, half on a brick at the bottom and there was hardly enough water to float a ping-pong ball.

"How nice to see the sun again," Mummy said. "No, it's not," said Wallace. "*I* want it to rain!"

Wallace's Seaside

"We're going to the seaside tomorrow, Henry," said Wallace one night as they settled down to sleep. "I'm going to swim."

"Me too," said Henry.

"And make a sand car," said Wallace.

But in the morning Henry wasn't feeling at all well. Mummy took him to the doctor who said he had german measles.

"Poor old Henry," said Mummy.

"Can we go to the seaside now?" asked Wallace as Mummy make Henry a hot drink.

"No, Wallace, we can't go to the sea with Henry ill."

Wallace began to cry. "I *do* want to go to the sea."

"I know but we can't," said Mummy. "I'm sorry, Wallace. We'll have to wait till Henry is better."

Wallace began to get angry; he rolled on the floor and kicked.

"You can play in the sand-pit," said Daddy.

"I don't *want* to play in the sand-pit."

"I'll get the paddling pool out for you."

"I don't *want* to go in the paddling pool."

"What a pity," said Daddy. 'I'm going to get it out anyway to clean it. Do you want to help?"

"No!" said Wallace, but he went out when he saw Daddy going to fetch it.

It still had sand in it from the last time he used it. Wallace carried his side quite easily. But first they had to put polythene underneath it to protect it from any sharp little stones on the terrace.

Then they filled buckets from the greenhouse tap. That was interesting. Wallace could work the tap — he could make it go full, make it go half and make it stop. It was heavy work carrying the cans, though. Daddy put some hot water in the pool.

Suddenly Wallace burst into tears again.

"What's the matter now?" asked Daddy.

"I want it next to the *tree*!"

Daddy moved the paddling pool next to the tree.

Then Wallace changed into his swimming pants; they were orange with blue dolphins on.

Mummy had got him some boats: there was the duck boat, and the plastic boat with three boats trailing behind it, and the wooden boat. Wallace was nicely settled now.

"Dad?"

"Yes, Wallace?"

"Will you go away, please?"

Daddy went away. Wallace fetched a few other things — plastic things that it wouldn't matter getting wet — and had a good time in the paddling pool.

After a while Daddy came out to drink his coffee.

"Dad, will you get a diving-board, please?"

Daddy got a piece of wood. It was a good one. First it was a diving-board for Robin Hood and Little John. Then it was a ramp for the orange snail. Then it fell right in and became a boat. It was one of the best boats because it didn't turn over and there was plenty of room for everybody: there was Duck — with his own boats too — Little John, Robin Hood, tyrannosaurus, the snail and the pig.

Then Wallace got a bucket from the sand-pit. He filled it up with water and carried it to the tree just beside the terrace. He poured some water on the truck. Then he got some more and climbed up into the tree, holding the bucket. That was difficult but he managed one bucketful.

"What are you putting water on the tree for?" asked Daddy, who was drinking his coffee nearby.

"To help you climb it," said Wallace. Daddy didn't say any more.

The next bucketful Wallace hung on the stump of a branch so that he could climb up into the tree and collect the bucket when he was up there. "I'm Tarzan," he said and shook the tree. When he reached down for the bucket he slipped and he and the bucket fell down onto the lawn, the bucket splashing water all over the terrace.

"Oh dear!" said Daddy, "did you fall, Tarzan?"

"No — I jumped," said Wallace, and he took a run at the paddling pool but his toe caught on the top of the side and he went plunging head first into the water, splashing Daddy on the other side.

"That was a good idea," said Daddy.

"Yes," said Wallace. He wiped the water out of his eyes. "It's a bit cold in here now, Dad — can you get some more hot water?"

"The sun's gone in," said Daddy. "Come on, I'll dry you."

"That was as good as a swim," said Wallace. "Will you make me a sand car now, Dad?"

"All right." Daddy set to work in the sand-pit. First he made a nice, flat, hard seat. Then he built up the panel with the dials and knobs, which were stones. Then he put in the plastic spade for a gearstick. Wallace climbed in and began to drive.

"Where are you going, Wallace?" Mummy called out of Henry's window.

"To the seaside!" Wallace shouted. "To the sea-side!"

And he drove and drove.

Fishing

Wallace decided to go fishing. So he got a piece of Daddy's bamboo from the garden and Mummy tied a piece of twine on the end.

Wallace fished everywhere: he fished out of his bunk bed and over the banisters; he fished off his rope ladder and he fished down the kitchen drain. Sometimes he caught Wussy if Wussy was feeling playful.

Then he asked Mum for a sock.

"What for?" Mum asked.

"Fishing," said Wallace.

Mummy found one of Daddy's old football stockings and threaded it onto the twine. It was a good shape for holding a fish in. Sometimes Wallace put things in the stocking and pretended he'd made a catch. And once when it rained very hard Wallace sat in the porch and held his rod and stocking out in the rain.

One day Wallace couldn't find his fishing rod. Mummy told him he'd left it in the car.

"And Daddy's got the car," said Wallace.

But when Daddy came back he told Wallace he had a surprise for him.

"Come and look at your fishing rod," he said.

Daddy took it out of the car and gave it to Wallace
to hold. It felt heavy.

"*What's* in the sock?" asked Wallace.

"Why, a fish, of course," said Daddy. "Have a
look."

"You show me," said Wallace.

Daddy put his hand into the sock and pulled out —
a fish!

"Cor!" said Wallace. "Hey, Mum, look — Daddy's
caught a fish. Where did you get it, Dad?"

And Daddy had to say he hadn't actually caught
it — Uncle Robert had.

"Uncle Robert? Does he go fishing *really*?"
asked Wallace.

"Certainly — perhaps he'll take you one day when
you're bigger. He might teach you how to fish —
really."

But Wallace wanted to go very soon. "Just to
watch," he said.

So they rang up Uncle Robert and he said

Wallace could come with him the next time he went.

"You'll have to be very patient," Daddy said. "And very quiet."

"I will be," said Wallace.

He was very excited when Uncle Robert came and took him to the lake where he fished. Uncle Robert had a real rod that came to bits and line and hooks and bait and little tins with things in them and floats and a reel and a bag and a net. Wallace carried the net.

When they had got to the landing stage where they fished from, it seemed to take Uncle Robert a long time to get everything ready. But in the end he flung out the line and the little red float which bobbed on the water. Then nothing happened. Uncle Robert just sat there, looking at the float.

"Haven't you caught anything yet?" asked Wallace.

Uncle Robert laughed. "You'll have to wait a lot longer than this," he said.

And Wallace *did* wait. He waited and waited: he looked at the clouds, he counted the ducks under the willow tree. Uncle Robert told him he must be quiet and still so Wallace only had thinking to do. After a while Uncle Robert pulled out the line.

"Have you got something?" said Wallace.

"No, no," said Uncle Robert, and Wallace could see the float in the air and the hook with its worm on. "Just checking the wom's still there," said Uncle Robert, " – thought I felt a bit of nibbling."

He swung the line out again, and bait and float fell lightly on the water.

After another while Uncle Robert said, "I'm not sure they're going for worms today. Here, Wallace, you hold the rod a minute while I go and see what else I've got in the car that might tempt them."

Suddenly Wallace felt very nervous at the thought of holding the rod but he sat down in Uncle Robert's place and took it in his hands.

"Now keep your eyes on the float *all* the time," said Uncle Robert. "If it goes under water jerk the rod up sharply — but not too sharp — and call for me. OK? And don't let the rod end droop into the water."

Wallace was left alone. He stared at that red float. The ripples on the surface of the water made it look as if it was moving through them. After a while Wallace thought it would make him giddy just watching the float and the ripples all the time: he might fall in. He glanced up to look at the ducks under the willow.

At that very moment he felt a jerk under his hands. Wallace almost let go of the rod in fright. He instantly looked back at the float. But . . . where was it? Wallace strained his eyes desperately all over the water in front of him: no float — it had disappeared. The line? He saw that all right, going straight down into the water. Then the float must be . . . Wallace jerked at the rod just as Uncle Robert had told him — up came the float and up came . . . a fish! Yes, a bright fish on the end of his line.

Wallace shouted for Uncle Robert but he was already beside him helping him swing the fish in.

"A perch!" he said. "Look at his prickly fins!"

"Will we eat *that*?" said Wallace, looking at the fish's black stripes and staring live eyes.

Uncle Robert carefully took the hook out of the fish's mouth and held it wriggling in his hand.

"We won't eat him," said Uncle Robert, "because he's too small — though he's a mighty good size for a first catch, Wallace." He put his hand in the water and let the fish go.

Soon after that Wallace's daddy came and took him home for lunch while Uncle Robert stayed at the lake, fishing.

In the evening Uncle Robert called by and showed Wallace the day's catch: two fine perch — much bigger than Wallace's. Uncle Robert gave Wallace one.

"One for the fish *you* caught," he said.

Wallace fetched his own rod and put the fish in the stocking. Then he presented it to Mummy for cooking.

Wallace and the Footballs

Wallace didn't want to go out to lunch at Matthew's house. He wanted to stay at home playing football.

"We're going *now*," said Mummy. But Wallace carried on kicking his ball about on the lawn. Daddy started the car to make Wallace understand.

Then they heard Wallace burst into tears.

"Silly boy!" muttered Daddy, and went to fetch him. But Wallace wasn't crying because he had to go: he was crying because his lovely new white football was punctured on a rose bush.

"If you'd come when we called that wouldn't have happened," said Daddy crossly.

"Stupid roses!" cried Wallace in a rage.

"Well, Matthew will probably have a ball," said Mummy, "you can play with him."

"I want my *own* ball," Wallace wailed.

Matthew lived in London in a house beside the river Thames and he didn't have a garden — or rather the garden was too small to play football in. Besides, Matthew didn't have a football. But they could look over the railing at the end of the garden down at the river. It was low tide and there was lots of mud.

"You couldn't play football in that mud very well," said Wallace.

During lunch the tide rose.

"I think they're going to have a sailing race this afternoon," said Matthew's mummy.

There was a motor boat chugging around on the river dropping huge orange balls over the side. "Marker buoys," said Daddy. But they just made Wallace think of footballs.

After lunch they went out to watch the boats. There was a big terrace on the riverside with a climbing frame in the shape of a helicopter and a slide and also an open space for children's games. At the end of the terrace there was a little shop selling ice-creams and toys. But it also had — hanging up in a big bag outside the door — lots of footballs, the black and white check sort, just what Wallace wanted.

"Oh Dad!" he said, and Daddy bought one for him. "There aren't any roses to burst this one on, are there, Dad?"

"No," said Daddy, "but there's the river — mind you keep the ball on the terrace."

So Wallace and Matthew had a good game on the terrace while the others leant on the wall and watched the boats.

But then Wallace got too excited and kicked the ball too hard — it went over Matthew's head, just hit the terrace wall, bounced up in the air and got taken by the wind over the wall and down onto the river.

"Oh no!" said Daddy, "there goes another one!"

"It'll be in the North Sea by morning," said Matthew's daddy.

"Couldn't we go in a boat and get it?" asked Wallace.

The ball was bobbing gently on the water, not going anywhere.

"We haven't got a boat," said Matthew's mummy. "But look — there's one of the sailing boats coming over — he might pick it up."

"Not easy," said Daddy.

A light blue boat with a beautiful white sail was gliding over the water in the direction of the ball. Wallace jumped up and down and waved and pointed at the ball and shouted to the two men in the boat. One of them looked up. As the boat ran beside the ball he leaned one arm over and scooped it up. Then he waved, the boat went about and sailed off across the river again.

"Get the number on the sail, Wallace," said Daddy, "and watch him."

Soon they had lost their boat amongst the many

others but they remembered the number. When the sailing boats came in from their race Wallace and the others were down at the quay waiting. Wallace thanked the man for picking his ball up.

"You were lucky," said the man.

When Wallace got home that day he played with his new ball on the lawn.

"Dad," he said, "can you move the roses?"

"No," said Daddy, "I *cannot* move the roses."

"Oh!" said Wallace, "I suppose I'll just have to be careful where I'm kicking the ball, won't I?"

"That's right," said Daddy, "you will."

A Night in the Woods

Daddy took Wallace and Henry into the woods to collect logs for the Guy Fawkes bonfire. The leaves were yellow on the trees and yellow on the ground. With each gust of wind more leaves showered down and Wallace and Henry tried to catch them as they fell.

"We could build a house here," said Wallace. "Dad, let's build a house!"

So Daddy got big branches — some of them taller than himself — and made them into a sort of wigwam round a group of little trees. Henry brought small branches and Wallace got leafy ones.

"Good for keeping off the rain," said Wallace. The best thing they found was an old door.

They gathered a big pile of dry yellow leaves. Then they all got inside and sat down.

"Mighty snug," said Daddy.

"We could have a picnic here," said Wallace.

"But not today," said Daddy. "It's getting dark."

"Dark!" said Henry. "The foxes will come."

They gathered up their Guy Fawkes logs and took them back to the house.

"We can have a picnic tomorrow," said Daddy. So the next day they *did* have a picnic. Mummy gave them a basket with a bottle of orange and three plastic cups; and a plastic box with garibaldis and ginger nuts in.

"That's not very much," said Wallace.

"It'll do for a picnic," said Mummy. "Now don't be out too long — come back before it gets dark, won't you?"

"Yes," said Daddy.

And off they went into the woods.

"We could play Tarzan here," said Wallace. "Daddy be Tarzan."

They put the basket in the house and ran about for a while playing Tarzan. Henry was Chita the chimpanzee. They found an old rope hanging from a branch which Wallace swung on, but Henry couldn't hold onto it very well so Daddy had to hold him on.

Then they went into their house and had their picnic.

"If we really were Tarzans we would sleep here, I should think," said Wallace.

"Monkeys would sleep here," said Henry.

"These leaves are as good as a sleeping-bag," said Wallace, and he lay down. "No, not enough," he said. "Come on, Daddy, let's get some more leaves."

So they piled more in.

"Now we can lie down," said Wallace.

"What about supper?" said Henry.

"We don't need supper," said Wallace.

"Don't need pyjamas," said Daddy.

"We don't have to clean our teeth," said Henry.

"We haven't got a book so we can't have a story,"

said Wallace. "Daddy tell us a story." So Daddy told them a story about a boy who went into the woods to find mushrooms for his granny and it got dark and he had to sleep in an old hollow tree while the owls hooted above his head.

They lay down in the leaves and went quiet. They could hear the cars passing on the road.

"Are you asleep, Daddy?" said Wallace.

"No," said Daddy, "Henry's wriggling on me."

"It's getting a bit dark," said Wallace.

The cars on the road had their lights on.

"The foxes'll be coming out soon, Henry," said Wallace.

"Come on, Dad," said Henry, "let's go home."

But just as they were scrambling out of their house something dark swooshed past them and they scrambled back in again.

"What was that?" said Wallace.

"I think it was an owl," said Daddy. "Can you hear it?"

"No," said Wallace.

But they could hear something else — footsteps.

"What's *that*?" whispered Wallace.

"I don't know," said Daddy.

Henry clung onto him. "Not foxes is it?" he said. The footsteps came closer. Then a voice said, "Anybody here, I wonder?" It was Mummy's voice.

"Ssshhh," said Wallace to Daddy and Henry, "pretend we're not here."

Henry giggled.

"Well," said Mummy's voice, "I thought Daddy

and Wallace and Henry would be somewhere around here. They don't mind spending the night with owls and foxes, I don't suppose."

Wallace and Henry scrambled out of the house and rushed at Mummy. "Help!" said Mummy, "the foxes are getting me." And they ran after her back to the house.

"Good gracious!" Mummy said when they were inside, "I thought you were going to be there all night."

"We did go to sleep," said Henry.

"Nearly," said Wallace.

They had a good hot bath with Daddy while Mummy made their supper.

"And where's the picnic basket?" Mummy asked.

"Oh dear!" said Daddy, "we left that behind."

"Well, we can't leave it there all night," said Mummy. "It'll get damp."

"The foxes'll take it," said Henry.

"I'll fetch it," said Daddy.

When he'd dressed he went out with the torch. It was quite dark. Wallace and Henry watched from the kitchen window as the torch went flashing into the wood.

"Daddy'll be all right by himself in the wood, I should think," said Wallace.

"In the dark," said Henry.

When Daddy came back he read them a story — a story that wasn't about woods or foxes or the dark. Then it was teeth-washing time and into bed. Wallace snuggled down.

"This is better than leaves," he said.

Mummy and Daddy kissed them both good night. In no time at all Henry was asleep. Outside the owl was hooting in the wood; inside the red nightlight was burning and Wallace wasn't afraid of anything.